PATROLLING POLICE CARS

To my neighbor, James Hughes—T.M.

KINGFISHER
LONDON & NEW YORK

Text copyright © Tony Mitton 2018
Illustrations copyright © Ant Parker 2018
Designed by Anthony Hannant (LittleRedAnt) 2018
Published in the United States by Kingfisher,
175 Fifth Ave., New York, NY 10010
Kingfisher is an imprint of Macmillan Children's Books, London.
All rights reserved.
Distributed in the U.S. and Canada by Macmillan, 175 Fifth Ave., New York, NY 10010

LIBRARY OF CONGRESS CATALOGING-IN-PUBLICATION DATA HAVE BEEN APPLIED FOR.

ISBN 978-0-7534-7455-6 (HB)
ISBN 978-0-7534-7456-3 (PB)

Kingfisher books are available for special promotions and premiums. For details contact:
Special Markets Department, Macmillan, 175 Fifth Ave., New York, NY 10010.

For more information, please visit
www.kingfisherbooks.com

Printed in China
9 8 7 6 5 4 3 2 1

PATROLLING POLICE CARS

Tony Mitton and

Ant Parker

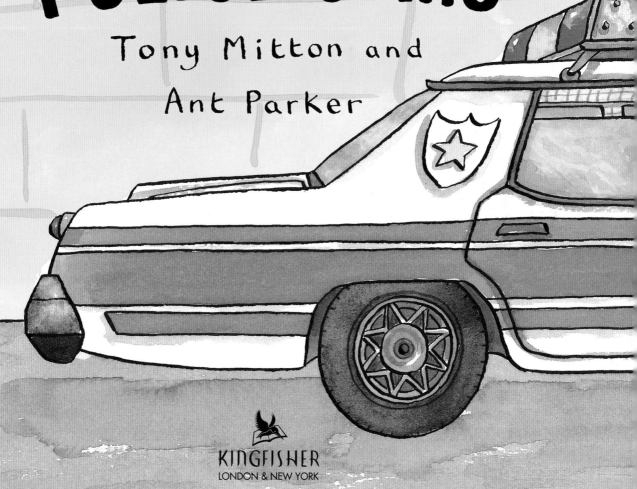

KINGFISHER

LONDON & NEW YORK

Patrolling almost anywhere,
in any neighborhood,

police cars help police keep all things
steady, safe, and good.

To get to an emergency
police cars sometimes need
to be there very quickly,
which means they have to speed.

To warn the other traffic
that they're going very fast
their flashing lights and sirens signal,
"Quickly, let me past!"

For giving them instructions
and to tell them where to go
the station contacts officers
by two-way radio.

Some cars have computers
that can use the Internet
to access all the information
that they need to get.

Police cars carry radars
to catch us if we're speeding.
They point them at a car
to get its speed shown as a reading.

When a car is going too fast
police can make it stop.
This car's getting cautioned by
a frowning traffic cop.

Police dogs use their sense of smell
to seek a person out.

This K-9 Unit's used to carry
dogs like this about.

When officers catch criminals
or suspects that they track,
they take them to the station
locked safely in the back.

Some cars have sheets of toughened glass
that firmly stand between
the front seats and the back seats,
to make a safety screen.

Police cars must be sturdy,
like these two that have made

an obstacle to block the road—
a two-car barricade!

Here's a tough push bumper.
When it's put in place
it helps police push heavy things
and clear away a space.

And here's a flexi-spotlight.
It shines a beam of light.
It's great for lighting up a scene—
it's powerful and bright.

Patrol cars have all kinds of things
they need to take around.
Neatly packed inside the trunk—
that's where they'll be found.

They even hold first aid kits,
so if you're hurt or bleeding
an officer can give you
the attention you'll be needing.

So when you see police cars,
as they cruise around,

remember that they're there for you,
to keep you safe and sound.

Police car bits

Siren
the loud sound draws attention to the flashing lights and tells people the police are coming

Flashing lights
these flash to warn other traffic to let the police car through

Flexi-Spotlight
this gives out a strong, bright light so work can be done in dark places

Safety screen
this separates the driver from passengers in the back

In-car computer
this allows police officers to get the information they need from the Internet

Push Bumper
this pushes away heavy obstacles and clears the way ahead